Where Magic Hides

Where Magic Hides

CAT WEATHERILL

To Chloe
Best Wishes
Cat Weatherill

Gomer

First published in 2019 by Gomer Press,
Llandysul, Ceredigion SA44 4JL

ISBN 978 1 78562 299 1

A CIP record for this title is available from the British Library.

This book is published with the financial support of the
Welsh Books Council.

Printed and bound in Wales at
Gomer Press, Llandysul, Ceredigion
www.gomer.co.uk

For Frank,
who goes fishing with nothing
on the end of his line

The Most
Beautiful Language
in the World

Long ago in Wales there lived a king who was worried. He was getting older and had no children.

'Who will be king after me?' he said to himself, as he sat in his chair by the fireside one night. 'I don't want people fighting over it. That would be terrible.'

He gazed into the flames and thought for a while. At last an idea came.

'A contest! That's what we need. But what kind of contest? Swords? Running? No, I am a King of Wales – it should be a *speaking* contest!' He slapped his thigh and grinned. 'Well done me, for thinking of it!'

The King went to bed a happy man. The next day, he gathered everyone together in the great hall of his castle. The fire was burning bright in the hearth. The dogs were sniffing beneath the tables for scraps. All the people of the court were waiting to hear what the King would say.

Finally, he rose to his feet.

'My friends,' he began. 'Who will be king, when I am gone? That is a troubling question. But we will soon know the answer! For I have decided: there will be a Grand Contest, and the winner shall be king after me.'

The hall became a babble of noise as everyone turned to their neighbour in astonishment. No one was expecting this! The King raised his arms to quieten them.

'Now, I *love* language,' he went on, 'and here in Wales we are blessed with a truly beautiful one. This is a land of song and story. We celebrate words. We honour our storytellers and verse-makers. And to hear our glorious Welsh language rolling on the tongue of a gifted speaker is mightily joyous to my ears.

'So, the contest is this: whoever speaks the most beautiful language shall be the winner. It is not the words that are important here. It is not a poetry competition. No, it is the *sound* of the language I will be judging. The rhythm of it. And most importantly of all, how it makes me feel when I hear it.

'There – it is done! Now my messengers shall travel across the land, telling people of the contest. And those same people will need time to travel here, to the castle. So I say this: we shall meet again, here in this very hall, in thirty days' time. Then the winner shall be chosen.'

The messengers rode out of the castle that same afternoon, their horses' hooves drumming the drawbridge as they went. They rode north, to the mountains of Snowdonia, and beyond, to the wild isle of Anglesey. They travelled east to the farms and fields of the borderlands. To the west, to the rolling sea and rugged cliffs. To the south, to the great settlement towns along the coast.

They visited every castle, to talk to the poets and storytellers employed there. But they also gave the message to the ordinary working folk, because not every poet wants to work in a castle. Some are happier speaking beneath the stars, sitting by a campfire. The King wanted everyone to know they were welcome: young or old, rich or poor, man or woman, master or beginner.

Soon the contestants began to arrive at the castle. The great walls around the courtyard rang to the rhythm of their words as they talked and practised. The competition day drew closer. The excitement bubbled like soup.

Finally, the day arrived. The King took his seat in the great hall and, one by one, the contestants stood before him. They recited poems and told stories long into the night, while the King closed his eyes and listened. Often, he smiled. Words flowed from mouths like mountain streams, sparkling and dancing. They rose, soft as morning mist over the fields. They flew through the air, fast and dark as bats at midnight. They snailed, slow and true, leaving their silver behind them.

The King enjoyed them all enormously. But when the end of the first day came, he yawned and went to bed without anyone being chosen as a winner. The second day was exactly the same. The third day began, as usual, with the King listening from his chair. He was incredibly patient. He never showed boredom and was very polite to everyone who had come.

Another young poet stepped forward to try his luck.

'Your Majesty,' he said, taking a deep breath to

steady his nerves. 'My name is Gwillim
from Brecon. This is a love poem I wrote

'Excellent,' said the King. 'Please – be

The young poet began. He had a ple
and spoke with great feeling. The King eased back
into his chair and closed his eyes. He could hear love
and warmth, a little hope, but...

The King's brow creased. Someone was talking.
Talking, while this young man was trying to do his
best. How rude!

The King opened his eyes and scanned the room.
To his right, several people had their backs turned to
him. They were clearly trying to quieten someone.

Then he heard a sudden loud noise. A strange,
gurgling kind of sound. One man stepped back. And
out from the crowd came a child, no more than two
years old. A boy, with a mop of pretty dark curls
on his head. He went towards the poet, wobbly as a
newborn lamb.

'Daddle ba,' said the baby. 'Caa. CAA!' He seized
hold of Gwillim's leg and hung on.

The poet tried gently to push him away, as a young
woman came out of the crowd. She was bent almost

ouble, trying not to be noticed. She shuffled forward and grabbed hold of the baby by his wrist.

'Come here,' she hissed under her breath. She tried to pull him free, but the baby had no desire to leave. Instead, he wrapped his other arm tight around the poet's knee.

'... *though my heart be ripped by thorns, my love is eternal...*' Gwillim tried to carry on.

'Come here!' said the woman, still tugging hard.

'Caa. CAAA!'

The King watched the tussle and began to smile. The toddler was so determined. He would not let go. The woman had turned bright pink with embarrassment and her cap had slid down over her eyes. The poet was flapping his arms, desperately trying to stay upright and finish his poem.

'... *as night follows day, so I follow thee...*'

The woman suddenly lost her balance and fell hard onto her backside with her skirts ruffled around her. The baby looked at her wide-eyed then began to laugh. The sound came up from his tummy and tumbled out of his mouth: a rich, infectious, happy, happy laugh.

'...*my love, my life...*'

The baby let go of Gwillim's leg and stood, swaying backwards and forwards. Then he turned and danced his way over to the King. Just as he neared the King's chair, he stumbled and fell forward. He put out his hands to save himself and ten sticky fingers landed on the rich fabric of the King's robe. People gasped.

The baby looked right into the King's eyes.

'G... g... gabaidle do?' he asked the King. 'Bach. Bach? Ca. Ca na fee. Da? DA?'

He waited for an answer. When nothing came, he shook his head then erupted into laughter once more.

'*Until the end of time,*' said Gwillim, and he dashed forward and swept the toddler up into his arms. 'I am so sorry, Your Majesty. He is my son. I told my wife to keep him outside.'

'He got away,' said the woman, picking herself up off the floor and rearranging her skirts.

'It's like trying to hold a salmon at spawning time.'

'No matter,' said the King. 'Put him down, Gwillim. He has done no harm.'

The poet put his son down. The baby sat on the stone floor, pulled off a sock and began to have a conversation with it. No words made any sense to anyone listening, and the baby couldn't control the volume of his own voice. Sometimes the words came out so loud, he surprised himself. When that happened, laughter followed.

'Amazing,' said the King, who was happily watching the baby play. 'It makes perfect sense to him. And to think I was like that once. As we all were. Soldier, poet, servant, King. We all begin the same.'

He smiled again and sighed deeply. 'It is, to me, a most joyous sound, this little one's language. It is pure. It comes straight from the heart. He speaks not to impress anyone, or trick or threaten anyone. I hear voices like that often here, in this hall. Any King would.

That is life.

'But this little man speaks only to make sense of his world. It is playful and true. It makes me feel young again, and hopeful. Peaceful. My world is brighter for hearing this sound.'

The King fell silent. Everyone could see he was thinking. Deciding. At last he rose to his feet.

'My friends,' he said. 'In the past few days, I have heard beautiful, beautiful language spoken. Some voices brought tears my eyes. Some made me believe

I could rule for ever. But I believe the most beautiful language came from this little chap here.'

He bent down and picked up the baby. 'Everyone – meet your future King.'

The whole room erupted. The baby had won? No! How?

The King's Advisor stepped forward. 'Your Majesty, I do not question your judgement. I simply speak for many of us when I say: he is only a child.'

'Yes, but he will grow. I am not planning on dying any time soon! I have plenty more years in me. He can be educated. And he has parents to help him. What is your day job, Gwillim?'

'I am a carpenter, Your Majesty. I have my own workshop.'

'Excellent. And you, Mrs Gwillim – I imagine your run your own household?'

'Yes, Your Majesty,' said the baby's mother, standing taller, 'and I do much more. I keep six goats and make the best cheese in Brecon. I am famous for it. My name is Bronwen.'

'See, Advisor?' said the King in delight. 'A man with the soul of a poet who can build things with his hands, and a woman who is successful in business.

Such people can build and run a country. What is the little one's name, by the way?'

'Harri, Your Majesty,' said the poet.

'King Harri! I like the sound of that,' said the King happily. He gently stroked Harri's soft cheek. 'I have a good feeling about this little chap. I think he will be a fine King one day.'

'Da!' said Harri with a grin. 'Da da DAA!'

Where Magic Hides

Megan Morgan was ten years old and loved Roald Dahl. She had read all his books. *Matilda* was her favourite.

Now her class was doing a Roald Dahl project for Book Week.

'He was born and grew up in Cardiff,' said Miss Hopkins, their teacher.

Megan was amazed. Her hand shot into the air. 'But Roald is not a Welsh name, Miss Hopkins.'

'You are right, Megan. Roald is a Norwegian name. His parents were from Norway. They named him after a famous Norwegian explorer, Roald Amundsen.'

Miss Hopkins held up a well-thumbed book. 'This is one of my favourites,' she said. '*Billy and the Minpins*. It talks about magic being all around us, and how we will see it if we believe in it.'

'That's rubbish, Miss!'

Aidan Jones was leaning back in his chair, grinning.

'It might have worked for him in Cardiff, but it wouldn't work here. There's no magic in Merthyr!'

Everyone laughed, even Miss Hopkins. Megan smiled. She had said exactly the same thing to her dada, four years before.

She had been six years old at the time, and mad about fairies.

Her bedroom was a rainbow explosion of dolls and unicorns, fairy tale books and trinkets. Wands, wings, flower headbands, glittery shoes... She loved it all.

There was only one thing Megan didn't have, and it was so important to her, she cried about it sometimes. She didn't have any magic. Real magic, the kind that makes your fingers tingle with excitement. And magic like that can't be bought.

It was Saturday morning. Megan was going to the supermarket with her dad, but it was raining. Again. She was wearing a fairy dress, and her wings got wet as she ran to the car.

One silver slipper slipped off and floated in a puddle.

Dada laughed when he saw her angry face. 'Come

on, Cinderella! Your carriage awaits!' He held open the car door. Megan clambered in.

Dada fished the soggy slipper out of the puddle and gave it to her. It dripped muddily onto Megan's dress. She took a deep breath and tried to keep calm.

'Don't let a bit of rain get you down,' said Dada. 'Rain makes things grow, so we need it, don't we?'

Megan said nothing.

'*Don't we?*' Dada was looking at her through the mirror.

'Yes,' she said. 'But I don't like it when it gets in the way.'

Dada laughed again. 'Fair enough!'

He drove out of their street and they began their journey out of Merthyr Tydfil. Megan gazed out of the window. Everything was grey. The lines of terraced houses, the railway bridge, the river, the factories... grey, grey, grey!

Soon they were on the Heads of the Valleys road, heading for the big supermarket on the hill.

'Look at that rain!' said Dada. It was sweeping across the valley like an army of ghosts.

The sky was thick and fleecy, slate grey.

Megan sighed.

'What's up, princess?'

'This,' said Megan, waving her hand at the whole scene. 'There's nothing here, Dada. Just... grey.'

'What are you looking for? Magic?'

Megan nodded.

'There's plenty of that here,' said Dada.

'Where?'

'Right here! There's magic in Merthyr, Megan. There's magic everywhere in Wales. The land is soaked with it. This is the land of dragons! They raced through the Valleys, once upon a time. Slept on the hills. Ate sheep by the hundred!

This is the land of Merlin. Now *he* was magic! And there were giants, and fairy women who came out of lakes and married mortal men. There were princes and princesses. Witches! They came across the sea from Ireland in a boat and landed on Anglesey. I read about it, love! I tell you – this place was a living fairy tale, long ago.'

'Maybe,' said Megan, 'but that was then. Fairies don't live here now. It's ugly and there's no magic anymore.'

'There is,' Dada insisted. 'You just don't get to see it, because you are always in bed at midnight.'

'*What?*'

'The magic in Merthyr happens at midnight. No, that's not quite right. It is here all the time, but it is easier to *see* it at midnight.'

Was Dada joking? Megan couldn't tell. 'Could I see it?'

'Course you could! One night I'll show you.'

Megan didn't believe him, though secretly she wished it was true. And she wondered: when would that night come?

It came a week later. Megan was fast asleep, so Dada woke her gently.

'It's time, princess, but you sleep on a bit. I'll wake you when we're there.'

He wrapped her in a blanket and carried her to the car. She lay down on the back seat and soon fell asleep.

When Dada woke her again, they were out of the town. He lifted her from the car and carried her, still wrapped in the blanket, to a wooden bench, then sat down and put her on his lap.

'Open your eyes, Meg.'

Sleepily, Megan did as he asked. 'Oh...!'

They were high above the town. The whole of

Merthyr lay spread out before them, like an enormous glittering blanket.

Factory lights, cinema lights, floodlights, house lights… So many lights, from dazzling white to soft gold. Road lights sparkled like necklaces. Crossing lights winked amber, on – off – on – off. Some lights were moving. Ambulance lights, flashing blue, heading to the hospital. Helicopter lights, warning red in the sky. Car headlights, scanning the roads like silver lizard eyes. And above them all, the shimmer of stars and a glorious, magical moon. 'Dada, it's... like fairyland.'

'I know. Do you believe fairies could live here now?'

'Oh yes. I am sure they do! I would, if I was a fairy.'

Dada looked at his watch. 'Listen.'

Megan listened. She could hear the wind in the trees behind them. A train, somewhere distant. A few cars. Then she heard it: a church bell, ringing out the hours of midnight.

She held her breath. Her heart was beating faster, she could feel it. Then her fingers began to tingle.

'Real magic,' she whispered.

Dada smiled. 'Just for you.'

Back in the classroom, Aidan was still arguing with Miss Hopkins.

'I tell you, nothing ever happens round here, Miss! Definitely not magic.'

Megan smiled. Let him think that! Roald Dahl was right: Aidan would never find where magic hides. But she had.

The Rainbow Village

Wil sat on the bench with his grandpa and gazed at the village green. *It looks exactly the same as last year,* he thought. He had been visiting Grampy every summer since he was little, and now he was eleven. Nothing ever changed.

'It's so quiet, Grampy,' he said. 'We could sit here all day and not see anyone.'

'That's because there's no one here any more, boy,' said Grampy, with a sigh. 'This place used to be full of life. We all had families once, but they've moved on. Your da is a good example. Went away to university in Cardiff, met your mam and never came back. Don't get me wrong – I'm happy for that. I know you have a wonderful life down there. But it makes it quiet here.' He took another bite of his sandwich. 'Everyone is the same. Every cottage you see has someone missing. Gwennie Next Door has a daughter in Australia. Geraint in the Old House has a son in Dubai. It wasn't like that for us. We all grew up in the village and stayed here.'

'The quiet is nice, though, isn't it, Grampy?' said Wil. 'I like it. Sometimes we go shopping in Cardiff on Saturday, and it is so full of people, you can hardly walk. Da hates it.'

Grampy smiled. 'I can imagine that! But there's good quiet and bad quiet, Wil. This village is dying. Everyone here is getting old, and when we die, these cottages will be bought by rich folk. And they won't live in 'em. They'll be holiday cottages. So if you sit here, in twenty years' time, on a cold November night, you'll see no lights on in any of these houses, because their owners will all be elsewhere, cosy in their big houses in London or wherever. This will be a ghost village.'

Wil's eyes widened. He suddenly had a vision of zombies lumbering down the lanes and a host of ghosts rising up out of their graves at midnight. But he knew it wasn't what Grampy meant. 'That's not good,' he said.

'No. A village must have life. Families growing up. New babies coming. A school. A village hall for dancing and music. Things to look forward to. People building futures together.'

'Is it really as bad as you are saying?'

'I fear so,' said Grampy.

Suddenly the day seemed darker. Wil had no idea how he could help. Maybe one day he would have the money to buy a house in the village, but by then it would be too late. He needed to do something now. But what?

The next day, it was raining, but he was too restless to stay in the house. His head was still full of everything Grampy had said.

'I need to get walking,' he said to himself. 'I always think better on my feet!'

He pulled on his boots and headed into the hills beyond the village. As he walked, he tried to find a way to help. Could he write to the politicians, back home in Cardiff? Would they listen to a ten-year-old boy?

He was so tangled up in the problem, he didn't notice when the rain stopped. He didn't see the clouds melt away. Didn't see the sky had turned deepest blue.

But he felt the ground begin to rumble beneath

his boots. Felt the electricity that sparked suddenly in the air around him. And he saw the rainbow that rose out of the ground ahead of him like the neck of a colossal diplodocus. Up, up, up it went – a vast band of light, heading for heaven – then down, down, down as it headed back to earth. And now the valley was spanned with a celestial bridge, shimmering and dancing, with the village lying directly beneath it.

Wil felt his whole body vibrating. 'It's so close,' he breathed. 'I could–' He said no more. He started running. Faster than he'd ever run in his life. And when he reached the rainbow, he threw himself inside before it could disappear.

Whoa, it was noisy! It sounded like the wind rustling through a thousand trees. There was no movement, just light. Thick bands of light, like stripes in an enormous squirt of toothpaste: red, orange, blue, purple, gold – GOLD!

Was it right there, beneath his feet? The pot of gold that lies at the end of every rainbow? There was only one way to find out!

Wil attacked the ground like a dog after a rabbit. He dug with his bare hands, on his knees. The soil sprayed out behind him.

'Come on, come on... yes! Oh YES!' He saw something glinting. He scraped away more dirt. A round edge... He grabbed hold and tugged hard.

A plate! A golden plate, like something from a Roman villa. There was writing on it:

Rainbows fade, as we must do
But wishes are forever true

What did it mean? Did it grant wishes? He turned the plate over. On the other side it said:

Wish wisely. Wish once. Wish now.

Wil looked up. Already the rainbow was fading. It was getting thin and wispy at the edges.

Wish, wish, wish! What did he want?

A gold Ferrari.

His own private jet.

Money! A bank full of money so he could buy every new video game that ever came out.

Oh, what did he want? Really, really want? In his heart? The rainbow was fading fast. He had to wish NOW.

He closed his eyes and listened hard. Waited for that little voice that whispered in his ear sometimes, telling him the best thing to do.

He heard it. He smiled. He held the plate tight in his hand and said:

'I want this village to be saved.'

BOOM!

The rainbow exploded above him. Suddenly it was raining – except it wasn't rain. It was huge drops of rainbow: red and yellow, pink and green... Every colour, falling down, soft as snow. And just like snow, it disappeared as soon as it touched something. Wil turned around and around, his arms outstretched, his head thrown back, feeling the drops kiss his fingers and face. He could taste them, sweet on his tongue. It was the most fantastic minute of his life. Because that was how long it lasted. Only a minute or so, then it was over. The rainbow, the plate – both were gone.

Suddenly Wil remembered the wish. Had it worked?

He ran back to the village, his heart pounding more with excitement than effort. What might he see? How would he know the wish had come true?

Climbing over the last gate, he stopped for a second

to catch his breath then jumped down and began to walk along the main road through the village. His eyes scanned from left to right, looking for some sign of change. Of magic. But there was nothing.

It was still deathly quiet. No new people. No voices or laughter. No music. No children. No babies crying.

Wil trudged home. He ate very little supper and had an early night. All his energy seemed to have left him. When he climbed into bed, his last thought was of the magic that hadn't worked.

'Ah well,' he said. 'I tried.'

Morning came. Wil looked at the clock on the bedside table. 5.35. It was already light outside. He stretched and went to the window. He pulled the curtains apart.

'What the...?!'

His bedroom overlooked one of Farmer Lewis's fields. It was full of sheep – and they were green. As green as the grass they were eating. Not only green. Some were red. Some were blue. Purple. Orange. Yellow.

'You're kidding me!'

Wil pulled on his shorts and trainers, raced downstairs, out of the house and into the lane.

He climbed over the gate into the farmer's field.

Up closer, he saw the sheep weren't coloured, it was their fleeces. They had been shorn for the summer, so the new fleeces were only just coming through. But the new wool was every colour of the rainbow.

'Oh my...!' Grampy came up behind him. 'Have you ever seen such a thing? How on earth can it have happened?'

'Actually, Grampy, I think it was me.' Wil told his grandpa the whole story.

'Owen! OWEN!'

Farmer Lewis was over the far side of the sheep field, waving at them. 'COME YER! COME SEE!'

Wil and Grampy crossed the field, the rainbow sheep scattering around them.

'This is quite some morning!' said the farmer as he took them into the farmyard. He pointed at his sheepdogs. They weren't black and white anymore. They were peacock blue.

'That's not all,' he said, and led the way into the milking shed. The cows were standing in their stalls as usual, munching mouthfuls of hay as the job was done. Wil saw they were orange and pink. But Farmer Lewis was pointing at the rubber tubes that carried the milk. It was rainbow milk!

'Ha! How does it taste?' said Grampy.

'Judge for yourself.' Farmer Lewis took up a jug and poured milk into two metal mugs.

Wil looked down into his mug. The milk swirled in every colour. He put it to his lips and drank.

'Ohhh!' The taste exploded on his tongue. It was more than delicious.

'My Beti is already making plans,' said the farmer. 'She wants a tea shop, selling rainbow cream cakes and ice cream! If you look, you'll see the pink cows are giving pink milk, the orange ones orange and so forth. So if we keep the milk separate, we could have it in different colours and add different flavours. Here she is now. Tell them, Bet.'

'It's a miracle,' said Beti. 'We have been struggling for so long, trying to keep the farm going. The wool was selling for next to nothing. The milk – well, you know, Owen, you read the papers. Price going down all the time. But this... People will come, can you imagine? Visitors. Tourists. We can open a tea room, an ice cream parlour... a gift shop! Sell milk, cream, yoghurt. All kinds of things. Owen – the village is saved.'

Her eyes turned silver with tears. Farmer Lewis gave her a cuddle.

Grampy had tears in his eyes too. 'Saved.' He put his arm around Wil's shoulders and pulled him close. '*Saved.*'

*   *   *

Four years went by. Wil was fourteen now. He sat in his mum's car as she drove them to the village, and noted all the changes.

The main road was still twisty and turny, and that pleased him. It hadn't been made straight and wide. The fields either side were full of farm animals, and it was a strange thing: they were the usual colour until his car drove over the village boundary. Then it was like someone had flipped a switch, because the next fields were full of rainbow sheep, rainbow cows and free-ranging rainbow chickens that laid rainbow-coloured eggs.

The village sign had changed. Now it said:

Pentref Yr Enfys
The Rainbow Village

The village had come alive. There were tourists on the main street, visiting the busy little businesses the villagers had set up. The Rainbow Tea Room. The Pink Palace Ice Cream Parlour. Yellow Goat Gifts.

The village pub had re-opened. It used to be the Green Dragon, but people thought it was risky to keep a name like that. No one was sure exactly how rainbow magic worked, and they didn't want a real dragon to swoop down suddenly out of the sky! So the pub had been re-named The Blue Sheepdog. The owners had three sky-blue collie dogs.

The biggest shop was Magical Yarns. It sold hand-knitted woollen clothes. Mrs Driscoll had started it, using local knitters and wool from the village sheep, but the demand was so great, she had to bring in fifteen more knitters to keep up. Two were from Croatia and one was from Poland. They knitted in a different style to the Welsh knitters, and Mrs Driscoll loved that. She also loved how they had moved into the village and brought their families with them.

So now the village had children and a new school. A village hall had been built.

When the magic had first happened, television news teams came from all around the world. Then the people began to come. Thousands of them! The press filled pages of newspapers and magazines with the story. Well, *most* of the story. There were only two people who knew how it happened, Wil and Grampy, and that was how they wanted it. Their secret.

Mum stopped the car outside Grampy's house. As Wil climbed out, the front door opened and there stood his grandpa. A little more wrinkly, but still the best grandpa in the world. Soon they were sitting in the kitchen. The tea pot was full. A newly-baked bara brith was waiting to be cut, with a dish of best blue butter beside it. Wil cut a thick slice and buttered it.

'Oh... heavenly!' he sighed, as the taste hit his tongue. 'I will never get tired of this!' He took a second bite. 'So Grampy – how are things?'

'Better than ever! Everyone is busy and very happy.'

Wil smiled. 'I am truly glad to hear that.'

The rain began as they chatted. Two hours later, as they returned to the car, they saw a huge rainbow in the sky above the village.

'I am so pleased you wished as you did,' said Grampy.

'So am I,' said Wil, 'though it could have been very different.'

'Really?'

'Oh yes. We could be getting into a gold Ferrari now!'

Grampy laughed. 'Then you'd better get chasing *that* rainbow, boy. RIGHT NOW!'

Never Cross the Bridge after Midnight

27 July 1997

Last night here. We move TOMORROW to Hay-on-Wye, the TOWN OF BOOKS. Mam says it has thirty-two bookshops!! Can't wait to explore them. Gonna need more pocket money, hahaha. Sleep now ... zzzzzzzzzzz...

'Please Mam. Please.'

'We need to get to the house,' his mam protested. 'We get the keys at one o'clock.'

Darren looked at the clock tower. 'That's half an hour away! Just one more.'

'Oh, okay,' said Mam. She pointed at a grocery shop. 'Look, I'll go in there and get some milk. Meet you here in five minutes. Goodness knows where your dad has gone.'

She disappeared into the shop, holding baby Huw tightly by the hand.

Darren grinned. He had been in five bookshops already, but was still hungry for more. Now he had spotted a black and white timbered shop, with cherry red window frames and a small black dog sitting outside. Time to explore! He crossed the road, patted the dog and slipped inside.

It was dark, and full of books. Hundreds of them, thousands of them, packed into heavy wooden bookcases, floor to ceiling. By the window, there was a small wooden desk with an old-fashioned cash till and a heavy, leather-bound ledger.

Who was minding the shop? Darren couldn't see anyone. But there was a door leading to another room, further back.

He walked through and found a second book-filled room, and then a third… and a fourth… and there, perched on a stool, was the strangest little man he had ever seen.

He was dressed completely in grey, with a grey handkerchief in his jacket pocket and old-fashioned grey lace-up boots. His face was thin, with a long pointed nose, pale grey eyes and a halo of grey hair.

He was no bigger than a ten year old and looked as dusty as his books.

His grey eyes blinked, once, twice. 'May I help you?' he asked, in a dry, papery voice.

'I'm just looking today,' said Darren. 'I don't have any money. But I will be back – I live here.' He felt a tummy-tingle of excitement as the words left his lips.

'You have just arrived,' said the small grey man, 'yet already you have been in five bookshops.' Somehow it was a statement, not a question. 'You are welcome. It is a wonderful town, is it not? Especially for those who love books as you do.'

'I do love books! Especially books about explorers and archaeologists. I like reading about the Aztecs, ancient Egypt – things like that.'

'You will find plenty of books on those subjects in this town. Some shops are stuffed with history books. We all have our passions. My friend Nathaniel sells nothing but bibles. Old, old bibles.'

'Who would want to buy a tatty old bible?' asked Darren, genuinely puzzled.

'Collectors!' The small grey man leaned forward and lowered his voice, though there was no one else in the shop to hear him. 'If Nathaniel sold all the bibles in his shop right now, he would have well over a million pounds in his pocket.'

'No way!'

'Yes. Sometimes old things are very, very valuable.' The small grey man smiled. 'You will learn much about the Town of Books as you explore, young fellow. Enjoy. Read. Make new friends. Walk in the mountains. Play by the river. There's just one thing you must not do.' He raised a finger, thin as a stick. 'Never cross the bridge after midnight. Not on the night of a new moon.'

'Why?'

'You don't need to know that. Just stay away. Now, go. Your mother is waiting for you.'

Darren thought often about the small grey man in the week that followed. How did he know he had moved to Hay? How did he know Mam was waiting? And most of all, what was so dangerous about the bridge?

He returned twice to the shop to see if the man was there, but he wasn't. The old desk had gone, the cash till was electric, and a perfectly ordinary-looking woman was serving.

It was all very odd.

5 August 1997
New moon TOMORROW. I am going to the
bridge. AFTER MIDNIGHT!!! Wish me luck...

The night of the new moon arrived. Darren waited
till everyone was asleep, then climbed out of bed and
pulled on his clothes. He slipped his torch into his
pocket and crept downstairs in his socks, carrying his
trainers, quietly, quietly, one step at a time. He put his
trainers on in the kitchen, opened the back door and
slipped into the garden like a cat.

Such a dark night! A new moon means no moon
at all, so he was glad he had the torch. He went down
the alley behind his house, along the high street, then
turned left onto the bridge road.

There was no one around. No people, no cars –
nothing. He looked at his watch: 2.15.

The bridge was coming closer. It looked safe. It was
wide and straight and empty. So why was his heart
hammering in his chest?

Just before the bridge, Darren turned off the torch.
There was nothing now except a thick, inky blackness.

He took a deep breath for courage and walked onto the bridge, keeping to the middle of the road.

Darren was on full alert. Any sound, any movement, he'd pick it up. He was sure of that. But he reached the far side of the bridge without anything happening.

Huh? He was relieved to get there but also disappointed. Had his courage been for nothing?

'That man was a trickster,' he muttered. 'There's nothing here.'

He turned for home. The night was still dark, but he had no fear now. This time, he walked on the pavement so he could look over the bridge.

He had only gone a little way when he heard a noise. A small splash, like something had fallen in below.

He turned on his torch, leaned over the bridge side and shone it down onto the riverbank below. Maybe it was the swans or–

'RRRRRRAAAAAA!'

An enormous hand appeared from nowhere, grabbed Darren by the scruff of the neck and hauled him off the bridge. He landed with a thump on the riverbank, the breath knocked clean out of his body.

He gasped, coughed, turned around – and saw a huge shape outlined against the night sky. An ogre, as tall as a double-decker bus with arms as long as trees.

Darren spun around on his bottom and looked for his torch. It was within reach and still shining. He grabbed it and shone it full on the ogre.

'Aaaaargh.' The ogre shielded his eyes with his arm. Darren saw he was bare-chested, deeply hairy, with a wide, flat head, an enormous mouth and tufts of dark hair sticking up on his head like beach grass.

The ogre roared again, and now his hand came out and seized hold of Darren, lifting him clean off the ground. He drew Darren closer to his mouth. Darren could smell old cheese, fish and cabbage, all mixed together in a stinky stew.

'Good evening, boy,' rumbled the giant.

'Put me down, Ogre!' said Darren, sounding braver than he felt.

'No ogre. Troll.'

'Whatever. You have no right to hold me like this, so PUT ME DOWN. I am a Welshman and you are only a troll.'

'Not only troll! Am Wye Valley Black-Backed Hairy Troll. And will pull head off– '

'NO! WAIT!' Darren was truly panicked. He thought trolls were brainless, grunting monsters, but this one clearly had his wits about him. If he was going to save his skin, he would have to think – fast. 'Just like that?' he said. 'With no sport before? I thought trolls liked games and riddles.'

The troll peered at him. His eyes were nut brown, like chimpanzee eyes. 'Had not finished speak,' he said. 'And you no Welshman.'

'I am! I was born in Swansea. I've lived there all my life till now. And I am eleven – that is a man in human terms. So finish speaking.'

The troll snorted. 'Was going say, will pull head off unless answer three questions.'

'That sounds fair enough,' said Darren. 'But put me down first. I can't think in mid-air.'

The troll looked unsure but set him down, then took hold of the hood of Darren's sweatshirt between his mighty finger and thumb, to stop him running away.

'Diolch,' said Darren. 'Now – shake on it.'

He offered the troll his hand. The troll pulled back. He had never been asked to do this before.

'Shake! Or the deal isn't done. Come on! I won't eat you.'

The troll took hold of Darren's hand and shook it.

'Right then,' said Darren. 'Let's begin. Unless you want to sit down first.'

'Why want sit down?'

'To be more comfortable,' said Darren. 'And that is your FIRST question gone!'

'No!' said the troll. 'No, no! Not play fair. Why do that?'

'Because I could. And that is your SECOND question gone!'

'NOOOO!' wailed the troll. 'NOOOO! You, me, can start again?'

'No, we can't. We shook on it. And that is your THIRD question gone!'

Darren did a victory dance, pumping the air with his fists and wagging his backside. The troll said nothing. He simply let go of Darren's hood then sat down on a nearby boulder. His shoulders slumped. He sighed. His whole body sagged until he looked like a worn-out armchair.

Suddenly Darren felt sorry for him. He couldn't help it. The troll looked so defeated.

'I'm sure something else will come over the bridge tonight,' he said. 'A lost sheep or something. You won't go hungry for long.'

'Not that,' said the troll. 'Not hungry. Just... had hope get some answer to things.'

'Really?' Now Darren was curious. 'What questions were you going to ask?'

'Well,' said the troll, livening up a bit. 'You seem clever lad. So wanted ask this: *why holly trees stay green in winter*?'

Darren frowned. 'I have no idea! That's a very good question. I know oak trees drop their leaves because they don't need them anymore, and it would put them at risk from winter winds if they kept them. But I don't know why other trees keep theirs. What was your second question?'

'Was: *why snowdrops come up in snow*? Why not wait spring, like more flowers?'

Darren thought for a moment. 'Again, I don't know. That's another really good question.

'So – what was your last one going to be?'

'*Why fingernails grow?*'

Darren smiled. He was *really* glad he had tricked the troll! His head would not be on his shoulders for much longer if they were really playing this game. 'I have no idea,' he admitted.

'Oh well,' said the troll with a deep sigh. 'Guess one day will find answer. Someone know.'

Darren thought for a moment. He really wanted to help. 'I know how we can find out!' he said at last. 'Hay is the Town of Books. The answer to all these questions will be there, in books.'

'What good that to me?' said the troll. 'No read.'

'But I can,' said Darren. 'We will do it together.'

The troll lifted his great head. 'Why do that for me?'

'Why would I not do it? You need help and I can give it.'

The troll's eyes widened. 'No one ever help me before. No one ever talk me. Honest! Come here three hundred years, night of new moon, never made no friend.'

Darren punched the troll's arm. 'You have one now.'

The very next day, Darren started searching for the answers. He went from bookshop to bookshop, and the owners were very helpful. They pulled books down from their shelves, gave him a seat and told him to read for as long as he needed. Not one of them asked him to buy a book.

Darren returned to the bridge on the night of the next new moon. He didn't have all the answers yet. But he had learned all kinds of fascinating things while searching, and the troll sat and listened like a little one being told a fairy tale. He loved every minute of it.

By spring, Darren and the troll knew the answers to all sorts of questions, and were the best of friends. Darren began to teach the troll how to read, and brought books from the library, so the troll could read in-between their meetings.

There was only one question they were never able to answer: *who was the small grey man*? The troll didn't know, and Darren never saw him again.

Though if *you* go to Hay-on-Wye – you might find him!

Snow Face

Danny threw himself backwards. The mighty armoured tail sliced through the air so close to his face, he felt the wind of its passing. Then came a terrible scraping sound as the dagger-long red claws ripped at the white scales of the other dragon. The white dragon flew into the air with a roar that seemed to rumble up from the belly of the earth. But the red dragon was upon him again. They clawed and tumbled and kicked and spat in the sky, while the king and his people watched and wailed.

Danny struggled to his feet. His back was bruised from the heavy fall. But he was smiling. He was right. Right! This was why the king couldn't build his castle. The dragons were fighting beneath it, night after night.

The king was striding towards him now, his arms outstretched. 'Young sir, I owe you an apology,' he said. 'When first you told of the dragons, I– '

'Danny! Get up!'

What?

'DANNY!'

'Ohhh….' Danny groaned as his dream fizzled into nothing. Was it seven o'clock already? He opened his eyes. Instantly he saw something was different in his bedroom. It was too light. Too quiet. Oh no…

'DANNY!'

He heard his mam racing up the stairs, coming for him like an excited puppy.

Oh NO…!

She exploded into his room. Even in the half light, he could see her face. Her Snow Face. Wide eyes, hands waving in the air, mouth open, almost too excited to speak.

'It's here!' she squealed.

'I kinda guessed.' Danny pulled the duvet closer to his chin.

'It's fantastic, isn't it?' Mam leapt over to the window and pulled the curtains wide open. A pale grey light flooded the bedroom: cold, strange, otherworldly. 'No school today.'

What?

Danny sat up in bed. 'Is that true?'

'It will be. Snow time!'

She started to dance. Her Happy Dance. That awful, bottom-wiggling, arm-punching dance she always did at moments like this. Danny hated it. She danced like a baby with its nappy off and didn't care who saw her.

'There's no school? Mam – do you know this for sure?'

'No. But look at it! There's tons of snow out there! They won't open the school today, Dan.'

'But the Animal Man was coming in today! He was bringing a fox. I've been waiting to see it for weeks.'

'You can see a fox anytime,' said Mam, waving the idea away. 'He'll come another day. But THIS...!' She turned back to the window, put both hands on the glass and gazed out. She sighed. Then she spun around, and there it was again. Her Snow Face. 'I have something for you!'

She ran out of the room and came back with an enormous something, wrapped in shiny blue paper.

'It's meant to be your birthday present,' she said. 'But I don't see the point of keeping it till then. It's snowing now. We might not have snow in January. Open it, Dan!'

He knew already what it was. Slowly he ripped off the paper. The sled lay on his lap, new, blue and totally unwanted.

Mam clapped her hands like a seal. 'Get dressed, and we'll get out there. Porridge?'

'Okay,' he grumbled. Mam kissed the top of his head and headed for the kitchen. 'And don't call me Porridge.'

*   *   *

Danny had all the gear. His mam had made sure of that. He would have liked new school shoes but Mam had spent the money on new welly boots. Then she had waved her plastic card to buy him thick socks... a puffy jacket... waterproof trousers... a woolly ski hat... gloves.

Mam was mad about snow. Nothing would stop her getting out into it. It could be polar cold, blowing a blizzard, real Walrus Weather (as she liked to call it). It made no difference. Snow was there to be played in, rolled in, enjoyed. And for some reason, she always wanted Danny to play with her. Why? He didn't like snow! Couldn't she see that? No, she couldn't. Sometimes she was like some wild older sister, more than a mam. Danny was always having to do things he didn't want to do. Go to places he didn't want to be, like Pen y Fan today.

Snow was cold and wet and boring. On a day like this, he would rather stay home with his books, computer and collection. He loved collecting skulls, feathers, fossils, bones... anything from the natural world. So he loved being outside – that wasn't the problem. The problem was the people. Today the mountains would be full of people just like Mam. Dozens of Snow Faces, throwing snowballs, making snowmen, and flying downhill on sleds, skis, metal trays – whatever they could find.

Danny liked to be on his own, exploring. Quiet. He couldn't explore today. Everything would be hidden under half a metre of snow. So he would rather read his new book. It was about Merlin, the cleverest wizard that had ever lived, and the ancient kings he worked with. King Vortigern the castle builder. King Uther Pendragon, father of King Arthur... Danny was loving it. His head was spinning with battles and magic.

Danny and his mam climbed the mountain

together, their breath steaming the air in front of them. That made Danny think of the dragons again, with their enormous wings and smoking mouths. He wished one would appear over the Beacons. That would send everyone running for home, haha!

Danny pulled the sled behind him. They weren't going to the top. There was no need. The local people knew, the slopes at the bottom were perfect for sledging.

Up and up they went, staying on the lane, then through the gate at the top. Danny's heart fell down into his new wellies. Yes, they were there. Loads of screaming people, wild with excitement. He could see some of his class mates. Olly was having a snowball fight with Noah and Jac. Their hair was dripping wet and their cheeks were red as tomatoes, but they didn't care.

'Owww!' howled Jac as another snowball hit him, hard. But he laughed too, then ran to Noah, pushed him over and started shoving snow into his jacket. Olly joined in and they all laughed like donkeys.

'Snow Faces,' muttered Danny.

Mam suddenly took hold of him by the elbow and led him to a clear bit of hill.

'This is perfect!' she said. 'You go first.'

Danny pulled a face.

'Come on! Show 'em how it's done.'

Danny decided to get on with it, in case she started Happy Dancing again.

He put the sled in place and sat on top. Mam pushed him from behind and voooosh! Away he went, hurtling down the hill, flying over the snow, faster and faster and faster. Everything was wind and whiteness. He couldn't see where the earth began or the sky ended. He could see there was no one ahead of him, so he gripped the rope harder, closed his eyes and lost himself in the speed of it all. Then he felt the sled slowing down and it was all over.

He stood up, turned and began the long trudge back up to Mam. She was just a tiny thing, jumping up and down, but he could see her holding one finger up to the sky. *Number 1, Number 1...*

Danny trudged on. Every footstep was an effort in the deep snow. Mam came down to help him once he was near the top. She couldn't wait to have a go herself.

'My turn,' she said and leapt on. Danny didn't need to push her. She got herself going: *voosh*! He watched her descend and waited while she climbed back up, dragging the sled behind her. She was much quicker coming up than he was, but still he had time to think...

'How fantastic is that?' she panted. 'This is a great sled. Very fast! Ready to go again?'

Danny took a deep breath. 'You know what, Mam? It was great, but I think you are enjoying it more than me. So you see that tree over there? The big oak? There's a huge stone under it. If I sat there, on the stone, you could see me – and I could watch you. Is that okay?'

Mam's eyes went wider than ever. 'You don't want another go? Are you kidding me?'

Danny shook his head. 'No, Mam. Honestly. I'm happy just to sit quiet and watch you having fun.'

Mam shook her head, but her eyes were diamond-bright. 'I don't know how you can say that. But if you're sure...'

'Yes, Mam. Yes. I'll be right there.' He pointed at the oak tree and started walking. He didn't look back, but he could feel his mam Happy Dancing behind him. Then he heard her cry of excitement as she took off again.

The oak was further away than it looked. Danny was out of breath by the time he reached it. He brushed the snow from the stone with his gloves then sat down. Now he was grateful for his waterproof trousers! The stone felt cold but not wet.

Danny loved this tree. The King's Tree he called it. Whenever he went exploring, he would sit here, on the King's Stone. Sometimes he ate his sandwiches here. Mam always gave him a bag of food to take.

'Adventurers need supplies,' she would say with a wink.

Danny could see her now, trekking back up the hill, keen for another go. He could see the Pavlova kids too. They lived in the house next door. Their dad was on his back in the snow, making a snow angel. Danny could hear the little kids' laughter, even from here.

So many people enjoying the snow. How many? Forty? Fifty? Maybe more.

Danny didn't know how he felt about this. Part of him wished he could join in and have easy fun like everyone else. So often he felt like the odd one out, watching everyone else doing things.

But another part of him was very happy. He was

doing what he liked to do. He didn't feel lonely. He didn't feel he was missing out. He felt he was very lucky. He had the time and space simply to be himself. To dream.

He gazed out from the stone. The world was very beautiful today. Somehow it looked bigger. Wilder. Above him rose the mountain, Pen y Fan, the highest peak in South Wales. Today it was sparkling silver, like it had been carved out of purest crystal. The sky had cleared to a sharp sapphire blue.

'My kingdom of ice,' he whispered.

He thought of Uther Pendragon and began to dream. He imagined he was a king too, in another time, another world, with an army of fearsome ice warriors. He could see them now, coming up the hill, with silver breastplates and cloaks made of wolfskin or bearskin. Heavy helmets, some with horns. Black leather boots. Leather gauntlets. Carrying all kinds of weapons. Danny loved longbows best.

Such fierce men needed fierce beasts. Danny gave them snow tigers, running free beside them. And now he imagined mammoths: twenty of them, with enormous curling tusks, tipped with silver. Their riders were sitting on immense saddles, swaying from side to side as the beasts strode through the snow.

The armour glinted in the clear sunshine. There were banners: red, blue, black. Someone was blowing a horn. Others came in reply. Someone was shouting: 'The king! The king!'

The whole army came to stand in front of him. Then, as he raised his hand, every warrior fell to his knees and bowed his head.

Danny grinned. He had never been a king before. He needed a name. King Daniel? No... That sounded like some kind of dog! He needed something older-sounding. Ah! He had it.

'Long live the king!' shouted one of the warriors. 'Long live King Macsen. Long live Macsen Snow Face.'

Danny grinned even wider. It wasn't such a bad day after all.

The Boy Who Went Fishing with Nothing on the End of his Line

'I don't understand,' said Elis. 'You are a vegetarian. You don't eat fish. So why are you going fishing?'

'Because I like it,' grinned Dylan.

The boys were in Beddgelert, standing outside Dylan's house. Dylan's bike was between them, with a fishing rod strapped to it.

'But don't you think it's cruel?' Elis went on. 'Using a hook? The fish's mouth can get ripped. I've seen it myself.'

Dylan nodded. 'Me too. So I am planning not to catch anything.'

Elis snorted. His best friend was always doing crazy things. That was why Elis liked him so much! Dylan was great fun to be around. But this made no sense. 'Why would anyone want to go fishing and not catch any fish?'

'Because I like the quiet,' said Dylan. 'I like the waiting. I like sitting on a rock in the sunshine, looking at the water. I don't need a fish flapping on the end of my line to make me happy.'

'But how are you going to stop that happening? How do you stop a fish taking the worm?'

'By not having a worm,' said Dylan. 'I will have a hook but nothing more.'

Elis laughed. 'You are crazy. Crazy! And where are you planning to do this?'

'Llyn Gwynant.'

Elis stopped laughing. 'Seriously? Llyn Gwynant? No.'

'Yes.'

'No! That's not a good idea. You know that. You'll hook a *llamhigyn y dwr*.'

'That's a myth,' said Dylan. 'Water leapers aren't real. Have you ever seen one?'

Elis shook his head. 'No, but that doesn't mean they don't exist. And everyone knows, Llyn Gwynant is their favourite lake.'

'I'm not scared.'

'You should be! They attack fishermen. Drag them down into the water and drown them. Sometimes they find empty fishing boats drifting on that lake. I tell you – you get a leaper on the end of your line and you're dead meat, boy.'

'I'm going,' said Dylan. 'Are you sure you won't come with me? Just for the ride? Mam's given me a ton of cheese sandwiches.'

'No,' said Elis. 'You're crazy.' He put his arm around his friend's shoulder. 'I'll miss you when you're dead.'

* * *

Dylan climbed onto the rocks at the far end of the lake, gazed at the clear sky and sighed happily. What a great day! The lake was so still, it was a perfect mirror. What a shame Elis hadn't come with him! It was strange... They usually did everything together. Dylan had never known his friend say no to an adventure.

He cast out his fishing line. *Pllpp.* The empty hook landed on the surface of the water and sank down.

Dylan thought about what his friend had said. He knew about the water leapers. For hundreds of years, if cattle or sheep were lost by the lake, the local farmers said the leapers had taken them. They stole the fish off lines too, and screamed if they were attacked.

But these were just stories.

Dylan reached for his bag and pulled out a sandwich. He began to chew. It always helped him think.

Why did people like to believe in such things? They weren't real. Why did they like to scare themselves silly? His friends did it all the time. Ghost stories, creepy movies... They loved to switch off the lights and imagine something bad was coming for them. A bogeyman under the bed. A ghost in the graveyard. A face in the mirror that wasn't their own. They loved all that kind of stuff. Dylan played along but didn't actually find it scary. He didn't have that kind of imagination.

An hour went by, then another. Still Dylan sat on the rocks, enjoying his day. He ate his sandwiches. Took off his trainers and socks and dangled his feet in the water. He made up a tune and hummed it a few times.

He didn't catch a fish. His plan was working, and that pleased him enormously. But at three o'clock, just as he was just thinking of going home, there was a sharp jerk on his fishing rod. Then another, so hard the rod was pulled right out of his hands. It slid across the rocks towards the water and he grabbed it just in time. He began to reel in the line. There was something struggling at the end of it.

'Oh no,' he groaned. 'I don't want this.'

The rod jerked hard in his hands as the fish fought to get free. It was clearly a strong one.

'I hope it's not a pike,' he muttered. Pike had extremely sharp teeth, like mini sharks. He knew it was almost impossible to get a hook out without killing them first. He decided he would cut the line if it was a pike. That wouldn't be good, leaving a hook in its mouth, but what else could he do?

The water was churning as the fish fought on. Still Dylan reeled in. It must be close now, he thought. He saw a sudden flash of silvery-green.

'Come on, come on...' He leaned back on his heels, trying to hold the rod. It was bending so hard, he thought it would snap. 'Come on... come on...'

And then *ffoosh*! Without warning, the fish flew out of the water and came right for him. Except it wasn't a fish – it was a water leaper. It looked like an enormous frog, but it didn't have front legs, it had wings. Flapping, leathery wings like a bat. And instead of back legs, it had a tail that ended in a sharp point with a stinger on the tip. The tail whipped sharply as the creature flew through the air, then stabbed Dylan in the neck. He felt a sting of pain as the poison went in. Then the leaper flew back to the water – still trailing the fishing line behind it – went beneath the surface and started to pull.

Dylan desperately tried to hold on to the rocks, but he was feeling woozy from the poison and his bare feet had no grip. The leaper was savage and strong, dragging him to his doom. Then more came. Dozens of water leapers, skimming across the surface of the lake, using their wings to haul themselves along. Their mouths were hanging open. He saw razor-sharp teeth, and long blue tongues that were tasting the air and finding – him! They howled in excitement. Their froggy eyes bulged to bursting and shone with an unnatural light. Dylan was powerless to stop them.

'Let go of the rod! LET GO OF THE ROD!'

Somewhere in his head, Dylan could hear a voice. Was it his own? Maybe. The poison was fogging his brain. He couldn't think anymore. He couldn't see much anymore.

'LET GO OF THE ROD! DYLAN! LET GO!'

Now there was someone coming across the rocks towards him. But the air was full of water leapers. They flew at him, wild and mean and determined. He tried to bat them away with his arm, but they were too strong and too many. He was going to die. He should have listened to Elis.

Elis. It was his friend who had hold of him now. Dylan felt the rod being ripped from his hands. Then he was gripped under the arms and pulled backwards. The leapers began to scream, a chorus of high-pitched shrieks that tore at his ears and made him want to jump into the lake to end the pain. But Elis was holding him, dragging him, saving him.

'Back off!' he was shouting. 'BACK OFF! You ain't havin' him! Not today!'

Then everything went purple and Dylan was unconscious.

When he awoke, he was lying on a grassy slope behind the rocks. His head throbbed. His neck pulsed with pain at the point where the stinger had gone in. But he was alive. Elis was sitting beside him.

'You came after me?' Dylan said weakly.

'Of course I did, you daft lump. I always have your back, don't I? And I had a bad feeling about this, soon as you said. So – do you believe in them now?'

Dylan began to nod but stopped almost immediately. It felt like his head was being rubbed by a cheese grater. 'Yes,' he managed.

'I don't think they liked you fishing with nothing on the end of your line,' said Elis. 'It was a bit like teasing.'

'Do you think I'm dying?' said Dylan. 'It feels like it.'

'No. I think you're just sick. But there's an ambulance coming. I phoned ten minutes ago. They should be here soon.'

'Thank you.' Dylan thought for a moment. 'Do you think they'll believe us?'

'I wasn't planning to tell them,' said Elis. 'I was going to say it was a snake. An adder. They are poisonous.'

'They might do blood tests, and find it's a different kind of poison, though?'

'Maybe. Maybe not. Do you really want to be mobbed by the TV people, Dyl? Cause that's what will happen if we tell them. They'll all be here, like a swarm of mozzies. And the police will want to ask questions, and...'

'I hear you,' said Dylan. 'Your story will do just fine.'

So they told the ambulance people Dylan had been bitten by a snake. The paramedic frowned a little when he looked at the wound. He was a local man and knew the stories. But he said nothing, simply looked at the lake for a moment.

'Quiet out there today,' he said. 'Nothing moving.' He filled a hypodermic syringe with anti-venom and pushed it into Dylan's arm. 'What bait were you using, boy?'

'Nothing. Just an empty hook.'

He nodded. And then he said, under his breath so the ambulance driver wouldn't hear: 'They wouldn't like that, you fishing with nothing on the end of your line. Don't do it again.'

'No sir,' said Dylan. 'Never.'

And he meant it.

Some Kind of Unicorn

Rhiannon left the farm and began the sharp climb up the hill behind her home. Ahead ran her dogs: lean, shaggy Bryn the lurcher and little Lottie, a shiny black terrier. They knew exactly where they were going. Rhiannon did this walk every day, no matter what the weather was doing. And here, high in the Powys hills, the weather did just about everything.

Some days they would walk beneath a huge bowl of blue sky. There would be no clouds, just a blazing sun and a pair of red kites, effortlessly circling. On other days, they would reach the top and the wind would be so strong, she was sure it would sweep her off her feet and carry her all the way to the sea.

Some days it rained so hard, it hurt. The rain would fly at them like pine needles. Bryn, with his thick coat, didn't mind. But little Lottie would blink as they hit her face, and slosh grumpily through the puddles.

Today Lottie was happy. The weather was fine. They would have a lovely walk over the high, rolling heathland.

Rhiannon loved living on the farm. She had such freedom. She was ten years old and allowed to walk the dogs on her own. How wonderful was that? She had a massive playground all to herself. No people, just sheep, rabbits, hares, foxes, birds and Welsh mountain ponies.

Rhiannon adored the ponies. They lived wild on the hills, all year round. They weren't tame. You couldn't pet them or feed them. They were wary of strangers and would run if anyone went close. They lived in family groups, one stallion and several mares. The mares usually had foals beside them. If not, they had huge round bellies with foals inside.

It was the stallion's job to keep the family safe. He was always alert. As soon as Rhiannon walked too close, he would snort, then swiftly trot away, proud and strong. Instantly, the females and foals would follow.

Rhiannon recognised five separate family groups

on her stretch of the hills. The ponies were short and sturdy, with very long manes and tails. Their coats were rougher and thicker than ridden ponies, and came in every colour. Brown, cream, grey, tan... Some were red as foxes. Some were like old-fashioned rocking horses, white with grey spots. Rhiannon thought they were wonderful. They looked magical. Mythical, like they had ridden out from the pages of an old, old book of stories. These ponies belonged to the land, the wind and the sky. To Wales itself.

When she saw them running across the hills, their long tails streaming behind them like smoke, her heart would fill with fierce excitement. Her breath would catch on her lips and her whole body would tingle. 'Run,' she would urge them. 'Run wild, run free, run forever.'

Rhiannon and the dogs walked on, following a narrow sheep trail. Lottie stayed close. She liked to explore the rabbit holes along the way. Bryn preferred to roam away from the path. He loved to chase hares. Rhiannon had read that a hare can run up to fifty miles an hour, so she never worried when he raced one. He wouldn't catch it!

Rhiannon watched him now as he picked his way

through a wet patch of ground then began to climb a ridge. The land here was empty, very up and down, with grass cropped short by sheep. There were no trees. Nothing was moving except a buzzard, flying low.

Bryn was sniffing the wind as he went. Suddenly he stopped and began to bark. It was short, sharp, quick, loud. Rhiannon knew what it meant: *Come*! I have found something.

Instantly Lottie raced to him, not wanting to miss out. Rhiannon followed more slowly. The ground was bumpy, and wet in places. Her boots kept getting stuck. Then she had to climb up the ridge.

Now Lottie was barking too.

'What? What? Hang on, I'm coming.'

Rhiannon sighed. It would probably be a dead sheep. Bryn often found them.

'Don't roll in it!' she shouted. He always did, and the smell was foul. Rotting meat. Yeuch! But he didn't usually bark at dead sheep. So what...?

'Hang on!' She moved faster, curious now. Over the boggy bit, up the ridge. 'What have you got? Oh my goodness!'

It was a foal. Its fur was red like autumn leaves.

But it was dead. It was lying on its side with its legs stretched straight out in front.

'Bryn! Come away! Lottie!'

Both dogs were snapping at it. It was terrible to see. 'BRYN! STOP IT.'

Rhiannon grabbed hold of Bryn's collar and dragged him away. And as she did, the foal moved. Its head lifted just a tiny amount and she saw its eyes were wide open.

'Oh! Bryn – stay. STAY. Lottie – LOTTIE! Come here. COME HERE. Now stay. Stay. STAY.'

The dogs reluctantly stayed a few metres away. Rhiannon went to the foal and crouched down beside it. She gently stroked its head. The fur behind its ears was super-soft. 'What has happened?' she said. 'Where's your mum?'

She stood up and looked around. She could see a long way. There was no sign of any ponies. 'Why has your mum left you? You'll die out here on your own. Have you broken your leg or something?'

She started examining the foal. How old was it? A week? It was much bigger than Bryn.

She ran her hands up and down the length of every leg. Nothing felt broken. There was no blood. The foal didn't seem feverish or in pain. It was just incredibly stiff. She couldn't get any leg to bend.

'You're like an ironing board! Look... let's try to get you onto your feet.'

She began to massage the foal's legs. She rubbed hard, trying to get some life back into the stiff limbs. After five minutes, she found she could bend one of the legs at the knee. Then another... and another... and another.

Feeling hopeful now, Rhiannon stood up and slid one arm under the foal's belly. The other she put over the top, like she was giving a bear hug. She hauled with all her strength and was able to get her knee under the foal's body to help support the weight.

'Yes! We can do this!'

Now she was able to slide her hands further under. She leaned in with her whole body and pushed, pushed, up, up... until the foal was upright, standing on all four legs.

'Yes! Well done, little feller!'

But he couldn't stand on his own. Rhiannon kept her arms around him to hold him up.

'What am I going to do with you now?'

She couldn't take the foal home with her – it

couldn't walk. She couldn't carry it. She could go home and fetch help, but if she took her hands away, it would fall back down, and while she was gone, the crows might take its eyes. She had seen that happen to sheep, and it was horrible. The foal had huge eyes, with long, long eyelashes. So beautiful. She couldn't let that happen.

Oh... where was its family?

Then it happened.

In that moment, in the middle of nowhere, with no one around to help, Rhiannon did a wondrous thing. She began to make a sound. She didn't think what she was doing. She did it by instinct. Out of her mouth came a long musical call. It was loud. It was lovely. It was pure and ancient. And she didn't stop. She just went on and on, filling the world with a call for help.

She sang with her voice, she sang with her heart. Her call rose and fell like a bird skimming over the hills. It flew beneath the endless grey sky, rippled the grass, hitched a ride on the back of the wind. It was urgent, true and magical.

And out of Rhiannon's sight, away over the next rise, it was heard. A pair of silvery-grey ears lifted to the sky and caught the call. And deep in his heart, a place older than time, the stallion understood.

Still Rhiannon sang, believing help would come. She never dreamed she'd see what happened next.

She heard the drumming of hooves. And from behind the next rise, the stallion came. Suddenly he was there, silhouetted against the sky. He was the colour of the moon, magical and magnificent, like some kind of unicorn. He whinnied.

Rhiannon called to him. 'Come here! Come here! I have your little one! Look! Look!' She could feel the foal moving beneath her. Now his dad was close, strength was returning to his little body.

'Come on!'

The stallion gazed at her intently, wise beyond words. He could see the dogs. Rhiannon knew he would never come with them so close.

'Wait! I'll take them.'

Was the foal able to stand on its own yet? Rhiannon relaxed her grip a little. It seemed possible.

She fully let go and returned to the dogs. She swept Lottie under one arm then took hold of Bryn's collar and firmly led him away.

'Come! Come!'

The foal was still standing, rigid as a table. The stallion waited until he judged the situation to be safe, then he swept down from the rise, head high, ears up, silver mane flying like a cloak. He went to the foal and sniffed it. Then he turned and trotted away, back up the rise to safety, with the foal trotting wobbly-legged behind him.

Rhiannon watched from a distance and found her eyes were brimming with tears. It was like a fairy tale. How had she done that? Found that voice, that call, that sound beyond words? How had she summoned such a glorious creature? That proud, wild stallion? She felt blessed. Enormously big yet small at the same time. Big because she had been a part of something so joyous. Small because the world seemed immense, packed with secrets only the animals and trees understood. She was only a human. Nothing special. But she had been allowed into their magical world for a few, breath-taking moments. Wow.

Rhiannon didn't notice the walk home. She danced along, dizzy with happiness. Her parents were both in the kitchen when she reached home. She began to tell them her story before she pulled her boots off.

'Oh, what a wonderful thing to happen,' sighed her

mum when she had finished. 'What sound did you make? I'm dying to know!'

'That's the weird thing,' said Rhiannon. 'I don't know. If you asked me to do it now, I couldn't. I can't begin to remember what I did or how it sounded. I just... opened my mouth and it came out. And it was really loud!'

'What a puzzle!' said her dad. 'But I am not entirely surprised. I think our brains are full of ancient knowledge – the old magic, if you like – and sometimes it comes out when we need it.'

'Maybe,' said her mum, thoughtfully. 'Or maybe it's because we named her Rhiannon.'

Dad grinned. 'The horse goddess!'

Rhiannon looked from one to the other. 'What do you mean? What horse goddess?'

'Rhiannon was a woman from the Otherworld,' explained her mum. 'She was very special. Intelligent, strong, magical... She married Pwyll, Prince of Dyfed. He was sitting on a magic mound when he first saw her. She was dressed in gold and riding on a dazzling white horse. So he fell madly in love with her, as princes do in these stories! He sent one of his men to bring her to him. But no one could catch her, though she seemed to be going slowly. It's Welsh mythology. We named you after her.'

'No way!' said Rhiannon. 'Why did you never tell me this? Where can I find this story? Why don't we have it?'

Her mum smiled and reached for a book on the top shelf of the dresser. 'We do. It's in here.'

She handed it to Rhiannon. It was heavy in her hands, and the pages of the cover felt grainy, like it was covered with the dust of many journeys.

Rhiannon read the title, *The Mabinogion*. She sighed happily. A thick book, full of adventure and magic. Perfect!

Cat is a performance storyteller, poet and best-selling author. She loves to travel the world, having adventures and making stories from them.

For seventeen years, she lived on a remote hill farm in the Radnorshire hills, not far from Hay on Wye. The landscape, folklore, myths and legends of Wales have always been a source of wonder and inspiration for her.

catweatherillauthor.com